He caught the next pitch on the nose. He really *drove* the ball to left. It climbed high and long, just the way his big homer had on Wednesday night.

Kenny leaped out of the box and charged toward first, but then he told himself to slow down. He was going to enjoy this one. A grand slam!

He went into his home-run trot, and waved his arms over his head.

But the wind held the ball up.

The left fielder had backed all the way to the fence, but now he came in a few steps. . .

Look for these books about the
Angel Park All-Stars

ROOKIE STAR

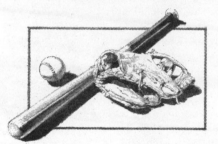

By Dean Hughes

Illustrated by Dennis Lyall

Bullseye Books • Alfred A. Knopf
New York

A BULLSEYE BOOK PUBLISHED BY ALFRED A. KNOPF, INC.
Copyright © 1990 by Dean Hughes
Cover art copyright © 1990 by Rick Ormond
Interior illustrations copyright © 1990 by Dennis Lyall
ANGEL PARK ALL-STARS characters copyright © 1989 by
Alfred A. Knopf, Inc.
Bullseye Books and Angel Park All-Stars are trademarks
of Alfred A. Knopf, Inc.

Library of Congress Cataloging-in-Publication Data
Hughes, Dean, 1943–
Rookie star / by Dean Hughes.
p.   cm. — (Angel Park all-stars ; #5)
Summary: Called "rookie star" by the town paper, third-grader
Kenny Sandoval, talented first baseman for the Angel Park Dodgers,
is determined to prove that the name has not gone to his head.
ISBN 0-679-90430-1 (lib. bdg.) — ISBN 0-679-80430-7 (pbk.)
[1. Baseball—Fiction. 2. Conduct of life—Fiction.] I. Title.
II. Series: Hughes, Dean, 1943– Angel Park all-stars ; 5.
PZ7.H87312Ro   1990
[Fic]—dc20   89-28877
CIP
AC

RL: 2:5
First Bullseye Books edition: July 1990
Manufactured in the United States of America
1   2   3   4   5   6   7   8   9   10

for Brett McKay

top
ers

no hits
victory
en runs,
d when
have a
coming
gs Giant
inal,
now that
be at his
Blue

ROOKIE STAR

Kenny Sandoval is only nine
Park Dodgers—but he plays li
his team to a victory over the S
did he drive in seven of thirtee
shortstop like a veteran. An
ble young S

Hot Night

Kenny Sandoval took one step and dove. He felt the baseball *slap* into the webbing of his glove.

He rolled over fast and came up to his knees. Then he gunned the ball to Jeff Reinhold, who was charging over to cover second base.

Oooouuuttt!!!!!!

Kenny jumped up. He gave Jeff a "thumbs up." Jeff flashed that broken-toothed grin of his.

But Kenny knew he had to get back to business. The force-out at second had left a fast runner on first.

The Dodgers were ahead, 6 to 2, but

Eddie Boschi was pitching, and he was struggling. Only good defense by the Dodgers had kept the Padres from scoring more.

Kenny watched Eddie stretch his long neck to look at the catcher. But when he wound up and pitched the ball, it didn't have much on it. It looped toward the batter and almost hit the plate.

Jim Cegielski, the Padres' catcher, almost swung, but he laid off in time.

The guy already had a double in the game, and Kenny could see that he was anxious for Eddie to get one up where he could hit it.

And Eddie did.

Cegielski pounded the ball hard on the ground. Jeff had to hurry to his left to make the pickup. As he did, Kenny ran toward the bag. "Second base," he yelled.

Jeff spun and threw, but the ball came in at Kenny's ankles. Kenny almost tripped as he reached low to grab it and then stretched to drag his foot across the bag.

Ooouuuuttt!!!!

Kenny caught his balance as he dug the

ball from his glove, and then he cocked and fired to Jenny Roper at first base.

Cegielski raced to beat the throw, and Jenny reached out as far as she could.

Bang. Bang.

Kenny wasn't sure.

And then he heard . . .

Ooooouuuuuuuuuttt!!!!!!

Double play!

Jeff and Kenny ran toward each other and jumped up for a big high-five, and then they both did the same with Jenny.

"Great play," she was shouting to both of them.

Little Brian Waters caught up with them as he ran in from right field. He pounded all three of them on the back. "I can't believe it. A double play!" he yelled.

Kenny felt good. All season they had been practicing double plays, but this was the first time they had turned one in a game.

And it was good timing. The Dodgers had won the first-half championship of their Little League, but to win the second half they had to play their best all the time.

The way Kenny was playing, maybe they

had no need to worry. In the first inning he had singled and scored on Rodney Bunson's double, and in the second he hit a double with the bases loaded.

It was a warm Southern California evening in late April. Kenny felt loose and strong . . . and *right*.

Coach Wilkens was waiting when his players ran to the dugout. He was smiling. "Hey, that was beee-*uuu*-tiful," he said.

Everyone came over and slapped hands with Kenny and Jeff and Jenny. Big Rodney Bunson yelled to the Padres, "Don't mess with *our* infield," and Sterling Malone, the Dodgers' center fielder, shouted, "That's just a start. We're going to eat you guys up."

Then Jenny went out and started the fourth inning by cracking a screecher of a line drive for a single.

That brought Kenny up.

He *knew* he was going to get another hit.

And when the ball came in, it was big as a full moon. Kenny swatted it with an easy motion, and the ball jumped off his bat.

It lifted high and long. It was still climbing when it sailed over the left fielder's head.

She turned, but she didn't take a step. She just watched it disappear over the fence.

Kenny wanted to do his home-run trot, but he was so excited that he almost caught up with Jenny.

As he stepped on home plate, he saw a woman crouching near the fence, taking his picture. He wondered who it was—but not for long. His whole team was waiting to slap his hand as he ran back to the dugout.

"What a *shot!*" Billy Bacon, the catcher, yelled. "That ball is still going. It's bouncing around scaring lizards out in the desert."

Everyone laughed.

And everyone got into the act.

Before the inning was over, the Dodgers had scored seven more runs and were ahead of the Padres, 13 to 2. Kenny had driven in two more runs himself. Now Eddie had all the lead he needed.

But Eddie still struggled.

In the bottom of the fourth he gave up a hit and a couple of walks, and then he walked a run home.

Eddie was disgusted with himself. He

kicked at the pitching rubber, and he talked to himself, but the next pitch floated up to the plate. The batter jumped on it and hit a hot shot that brought in another run.

Kenny knew the coach wanted three good pitchers, and he was trying to help Eddie improve. But Eddie was losing his cool tonight.

The coach came out and talked to him, and then took him out of the game. He called for Kenny to come to the mound.

It was Kenny's night.

He got two outs to end the inning, and then he retired the final six batters in order.

After the game he and the other Dodger rookies, Jacob Scott and Harlan Sloan, walked home together. Jacob had gotten a hit and an RBI. Harlan had walked with the bases loaded, and he had made some good plays at first.

All three of them were feeling good.

Jacob used his favorite big-league radio announcer's voice to describe the game. "Kenny Sandoval was a one-man wrecking crew tonight. He could have played the Padres *by himself*."

He grinned, showing the gap between his front teeth. He was a freckle-faced kid who could almost always make Kenny laugh.

But Kenny said, "Hey, don't say that. I just got lucky."

Big Harlan slapped Kenny on the back— harder than he really needed to. He had a way of doing things by accident. "That wasn't luck. That was great playing," he said.

And a local newspaper reporter agreed.

The next night, when Kenny came home from baseball practice, Kenny's mom said, "Take a look at the *Valley Sentinel*. There's a picture of you."

Sure enough. Kenny found himself, big as life, jumping on home plate with a big smile on his face. And next to the picture was an article about the game:

Rookie Star

Kenny Sandoval is only nine and a rookie for the Angel Park Dodgers—but he plays like a star. Last night he led his

team to a victory over the Santa Rita
Padres. Not only did he drive in seven
of thirteen runs, but he played shortstop
like a veteran. And when the starting
pitcher got himself in trouble, young
Sandoval came in and shut down the
Padres with no hits over the final two and
two-thirds innings.

Last week the Dodgers won the first-
half championship for their league, which
includes teams from towns throughout
the valley. The Dodgers seem to have a
good chance to go all the way this year
now that they have a player like Sandoval.
He will have to be at his best this coming
Saturday, when the Dodgers play the Blue
Springs Giants, one of the best teams in
the league.

Kenny comes by his ability naturally.
His father, a local electrical contractor,
once pitched for the big-league Dodgers
before arm trouble cut his career short.
When asked whether he hoped his son
could play major-league baseball someday, he replied, "Well, sure, but right now
I just want him to enjoy the game and
have some fun."

Maybe so. But Mr. Sandoval is too
modest. It would appear that he—and
Angel Park—will be watching Kenny

Sandoval for many years to come: and
not just in local leagues. He seems des-
tined for the big time. We'd be surprised
if the "rookie star" is not a World Series
star someday.

Kenny couldn't believe it. He put down
the paper and stared at his mother. She was
smiling, but Kenny wasn't.

"They shouldn't write stuff like that,"
Kenny said.

"Why not? It's all true."

"It makes me sound like I'm the whole
team. That's not true. Bunson's a better hitter *and* pitcher than I am."

"He's a sixth-grader. That reporter was
just saying you're great for a rookie. And
that's true."

"Yeah, but what about Jacob and Harlan?
How's that going to make them feel?"

Kenny got his answer right away.

The phone rang. Jacob was on the line.
"Hey, Kenny, *what a story!*"

"It was stupid," Kenny said.

"Why?"

"Hey, I do okay for my age—but that

doesn't mean I'll make it to the majors. That's a million years from now."

"Come on, Kenny, lay off the act. You *loved* reading about yourself."

Kenny was taken by surprise. He really had been happy when he saw his picture, but he *didn't* like the article. He was afraid of what the other Dodgers would think. And he knew players all over the league were going to be giving him a hard time.

"Jacob, I'm not putting on an act. I—"

"Hey, you're the *rookie star*. I hope you don't mind hanging around with us regular guys anymore."

"That's why I don't like the article, Jacob. Everybody's going to be saying stuff like that."

"You'll live," Jacob said.

That was just the tone Kenny didn't want to hear. He was afraid he was going to hear a lot more of it.

BOX SCORE, GAME 11

Angel Park Dodgers   13

	ab	r	h	rbi
White 3b	4	2	1	0
Roper 1b	2	3	2	0
Sandoval ss	4	3	4	7
Bunson lf	3	1	1	2
Malone cf	2	1	2	1
Reinhold 2b	4	1	1	1
Boschi p	3	0	0	0
Bacon c	3	1	0	0
Waters rf	2	0	1	0
Scott rf	2	1	1	1
Sloan 1b	1	0	0	1
Sandia ss	1	0	0	0
ttl	**31**	**13**	**13**	**13**

Santa Rita Padres   4

	ab	r	h	rbi
Roberts 2b	2	1	1	1
Blough 3b	3	0	1	0
Brown lf	3	0	0	0
Cegielski c	3	0	1	1
Jorgensen cf	1	1	0	0
Shimer rf	3	0	0	0
Durkin 1b	1	1	1	0
Kim p	2	0	1	0
Nakatani ss	2	0	1	2
Brenchley cf	1	0	0	0
Valenciano p	1	0	0	0
Orosco 1b	1	1	0	0
	23	**4**	**6**	**4**

Dodgers   2 4 0 7 0 0—13
Padres   1 1 0 2 0 0—4

★ 2 ★

Hot Dog

Coach Wilkens called that night, too. He mentioned the article and even congratulated Kenny, but he didn't make a big deal of it.

"Kenny, I'm concerned about something," he said. "But I've got to have your promise you won't tell *anyone* else about it."

"Sure. I won't say anything."

"Okay. I talked to Jenny after the game yesterday. She's doing a great job and having fun, but she said that it's tough sometimes to be the only girl. She feels left out a lot."

"I thought everyone just treated her the same."

"Well, they do at the games, but sometimes the guys her age get together to hold their own practices, and they never include her."

"I don't see why."

"I don't either. But I think they feel funny about calling a girl. I asked Jeff about it, and he said, 'If I call her, she'll think I'm trying to go with her.' "

Kenny thought he understood that.

"You could do it, though," Coach Wilkens said. "You're young enough that she wouldn't think anything about it."

"Yeah, but she might feel stupid going over to the park with a third-grader."

"Not with you, she wouldn't. You're the 'rookie star.' " The coach laughed a little.

"Coach, I wish the paper hadn't said that."

"Hey, I don't blame you. But you can't help what some reporter decided to write."

Kenny hoped the players on the team would think that way.

"So, anyway, would you mind giving Jenny a call sometime? Maybe you could get some other kids together, and just be the one to get Jenny involved."

"Okay. I guess I can do that."

But the coach didn't know how shy Kenny was about that sort of stuff. Kenny thought all evening about how he could do it.

He hated to invite her to practice with the rookies—because she might feel dumb with three third-graders. And he hated to call the older guys, because they might think he was acting like the "rookie star" all of a sudden.

Finally Kenny decided he would just ask Jenny if she would go to the park and catch some of his throws. Then once they got to the park, other guys might be there.

But he still couldn't get himself to call her.

He put it off all evening, until he decided that he would rather talk to her face-to-face and he would do that at school the next day.

Then he put it off all day.

When school got out, he knew he had to get up his nerve, so he walked over to her fifth-grade classroom and waited for her.

When she came out, however, she was with her two best friends. Kenny lost his nerve all over again until Jenny said, "Hi, Kenny."

One of her friends—a girl named Cindy, who was about half as tall as Jenny—said,

"Ooooh, Kenny, I saw your picture in the newspaper last night. You're the *star* of the team."

"No I'm not."

The girls laughed, but Jenny said, "Kenny's a good player. *Really* good."

She started to walk away.

"Jenny?"

"Yeah."

"I was wondering . . ." The other girls turned around, too.

"He wants to ask you on a date," Cindy said.

Jenny punched her on the shoulder. "Shut up, Cindy," she said.

"I just wondered if you could go over to the park with me sometime maybe, so I can sort of practice my throw to first," Kenny said.

He hadn't realized how stupid that would sound. His throws to first had been right on target.

Jenny gave him a funny look, as though she didn't quite believe him. "Why don't you throw to Harlan?" she asked. "He plays first base, too."

Oh.

Kenny hadn't thought of that. He suddenly knew he was in a real mess. He had to think of something to say.

"Well . . . yeah. But he's only learning. A lot of times he lets the ball get by him."

Jenny still looked doubtful. "Well, yeah. I can catch some for you. This isn't because . . ."

But she stopped.

Kenny looked at the floor.

"Well, okay," Jenny said. "Do you want to go over now?"

"Sure. I'll go home and change and get my glove—and I'll meet you over there."

"Oooooh-ooooooh," Cindy said. "It looks like Kenny's found himself a fifth-grade girlfriend."

"Shut *up*," Jenny said, and she took another swipe as Cindy jumped back.

Kenny got out of there.

When Kenny got to the park, he spotted some of the other players and joined them. He felt a lot more comfortable that way, and Jenny seemed happy about it, too.

So Kenny had done what the coach asked, and it had worked out.

He was relieved.

And then he saw Jacob and Harlan walking toward the diamond.

He usually practiced with them.

"Hey, come on over," Kenny yelled to them. "We're just going to start some infield practice."

But the boys kept walking straight toward Kenny. From the looks on their faces, something was wrong.

"What's going on?" Jacob asked.

"What do you mean?"

"I called your house, and your mom said you were coming over here."

"Yeah. Right."

"So why didn't you call us—or wait for us at school?"

"Oh. I don't know. I figured you'd show up, I guess."

Jacob wasn't buying that. He was staring at Kenny, and he still looked mad.

"Maybe you think you're too good to work out with little kids now that you're the *rookie star*."

"Come on, Jacob."

Kenny didn't know what to say. He couldn't really explain. He looked over at Harlan. Harlan didn't seem quite so angry, but he wasn't telling Jacob to stop either.

"Just come on and play," Kenny said.

"Oh, *gee*," Jacob said, and he looked at Harlan. "Isn't Kenny wonderful? He's such a *star*, and yet he doesn't mind playing with plain old *regular* rookies."

Kenny wanted to tell them about the coach calling. But he couldn't.

And so he said nothing.

Jacob and Harlan didn't even stay to practice. They walked away. And as they left, Jacob mumbled to Harlan, just loud enough for Kenny to hear, "Some guys don't remember their promises very long."

Kenny knew what that meant. The three of them had promised to stick together all season and help each other out.

Kenny wasn't going back on that. But what could he say?

Nothing. Kenny was in a bind, and there was nothing he could do but watch his two best friends leave. He hadn't felt so lousy in a long time.

★ 3 ★

Giant Mouths

The next morning was the big game with the Giants. But before long Kenny wasn't sure who his enemy was. The Giants were on him from the moment they spotted him, but so were some of his own teammates, and his two best friends wouldn't even talk to him.

What was he supposed to do?

Maybe he could make his friends understand about Jenny—sooner or later—but for right now he just had to play some great baseball and show everyone that he didn't have a big head.

But "Heat" Halliday, the Giants' super pitcher, was really popping his fastball. Henry White started out the game by striking out. And Sterling Malone popped up to the catcher.

When Kenny walked to the plate, he was telling himself he couldn't worry about any of that. He had gotten hits off Halliday before, and he could do it again.

But "Cranny" Crandall was waiting for Kenny. He stood up straight and lifted his catcher's mask. "What? Is it really *him*? Is it really the *rookie star*?"

Kenny ignored him. He tried to relax.

But Cranny couldn't let things go. "Hey, Heat," he yelled, "don't get scared, but the *rookie STAAARRRRR* is up. Whatever you do, don't make him fall down and get his uniform dirty."

Yeah, right, Kenny thought. Cranny was the kid who looked as though he *dragged* his uniform to the park—over a dirt road.

But Kenny said nothing. Maybe he smiled a little—just to bug Cranny.

And Billy Bacon shouted, "Hey, Cranny.

You *look* like a bag of potatoes. But you *smell* like the potatoes have turned rotten!"

Cranny didn't like that.

Maybe Heat didn't either.

Kenny was suddenly spinning away as the first pitch whizzed past his ribs.

"Oops," Cranny said. And then he yelled again, "Hey, Heat, be careful. You could hurt the little star."

But the ump didn't like that. He stepped out from behind the plate and said to Heat, "Young man, you'd better not be throwing at the batter on purpose."

"It got away from him," Cranny said.

He was grinning.

Kenny stepped out for a moment. There was a blustery wind, and it had blown something into his eye.

He wiped his eye and then dug back in at the plate. He even moved in a little closer. Halliday wasn't going to scare him. But on the next pitch Kenny caught himself bailing out, even though the ball was over the plate.

The umpire called it a strike.

Kenny got ready again. No way was he going to stand there and let another good pitch go by.

But he swung at a pitch that was low, and he fouled it away.

With two strikes, Heat just might come inside on him again.

But Heat threw his big curve that broke right across the plate. Kenny caught himself cringing, pulling back. But he swung.

And missed.

Halliday had outsmarted him all the way.

Kenny told himself he wouldn't let that happen next time. He ran back and got his glove, and then he headed for his position at shortstop.

The Giants were all yelling that the rookie star wasn't so hot after all. Kenny told himself not to listen. He would play tough defense and not worry about those guys.

But he didn't have to play defense. Bunson was throwing just as much heat as Halliday. He gave up a bloop single to the Giants' second batter, but then he struck out the shortstop and the center fielder, who were both good hitters.

Halliday also gave up a hit in the next inning—and a walk. Billy Bacon came up with a chance to do some damage, but he tried too hard.

Kenny could see that Cranny was mouthing off, as usual, and Billy was letting it bother him.

Billy fouled off three pitches, and then he swung with all he had and missed. As he walked away, he turned and told Cranny to shut his mouth.

Kenny ran back out to the field. He tossed the ball around with the infielders, but when he made a low throw to first, all the Giants started laughing and making fun of him again.

And maybe Kenny still had that on his mind when Cranny came up to bat with one out.

Crandall hit a soft grounder right at Kenny, and the ball came up just right. Kenny took the good hop and made the easy toss to first.

But he threw harder than he needed to.

The ball flew wide and Jenny had to spin around for it. It bounced off her glove and rolled into foul territory. By the time she chased it down, Cranny was standing on second.

And he was laughing.

"What's the trouble, *star*?" he said to Kenny. "I thought I read in the paper that you don't do stuff like that."

Kenny could live with that. What bothered him a lot more was that Jeff Reinhold looked over and said, "Come *on*, Kenny. Keep your mind on the game."

And when he looked toward the dugout, he saw Jacob and Harlan talking. He figured they were saying the same thing: Kenny had his head in the clouds now that he thought he was a "star."

But Kenny felt ten times worse when the Giants' first baseman hit a single to right. Cranny scored and the Giants were ahead.

The guy never should have been on base, Kenny told himself.

That was his own fault.

No more damage was done, but when Kenny walked off the field, his teammates were yelling, "Come on, let's get *serious*. Let's kick these guys."

Kenny was reading something into everything now. Did they think he wasn't serious? Did they think he hadn't been trying?

But things started looking better immediately. Brian Waters played it smart and laid down a perfect bunt. The play was close at first, but he beat it out.

Halliday got tough and struck out Henry again. But Malone fouled off a few pitches and finally worked Halliday for a walk.

Kenny came up this time with a chance to prove that he was giving his best.

The Giants had plenty to say, of course, and Granny never stopped.

Even one of the Giants' parents shouted, "Come on, Heat! Show him what you thought of that newspaper article."

Billy hollered, "He couldn't read it. The words were too big."

Kenny stepped out of the box. He tried

to shut it all out. "Concentrate," he said aloud, and he stepped back in.

But just then he heard Danny Sandia, his own teammate, yell, "Hey, Kenny, show us what rookie *stars* do."

Kenny tried.

He swung at the first pitch and got good wood on it. He drove the ball hard to left.

It was sinking fast as the left fielder charged.

But just when Kenny thought the ball was going to hit the grass, the left fielder dove and made a great catch.

Kenny's heart sank. He had to turn and trot back to the dugout.

Jenny yelled, "Good try, Kenny," but the Giants were all laughing and shouting insults.

As Kenny came into the dugout, Danny said, "Gee, I guess Bunson will have to be the hero. The rookie star couldn't do it."

A couple of players told Danny to lay off, but that didn't make Kenny feel much better. He sat down on the bench, alone—far from Jacob and Harlan.

And Bunson had no more luck than Kenny. He hit the ball high in the air. The left fielder got under it easily and made the catch.

The Dodgers were still down 1 to 0.

★ 4 ★

One Pitch

In the fifth inning the Dodgers finally got something going again. Heat Halliday got a little sloppy and walked Jacob. And then Henry poked a drive into right field for a single.

When Sterling came up, the Dodgers were yelling for him to blast one. The Dodgers had only had three hits all night, so everyone knew this might be their best chance to score.

Sterling took his helmet off and wiped his sleeve over his forehead and then back over his blocked hair. He wore his hair short on the sides and flat on top in a "fade," like a lot of the black guys were doing.

Sterling put his helmet back on. He looked serious.

But Heat was serious, too. He fired a hard fastball. Sterling took it, and the umpire called it a strike. Sterling stepped out of the box and shot a mean glance at the umpire.

But he didn't say anything.

He stepped back in, pulled his batting glove tight, and then he glared out at Halliday.

Heat changed up with a slow breaking ball. But Sterling timed it and *crunched* it.

The ball shot down the left field line and rolled to the fence.

Both runners scored. Sterling stopped at second.

The Dodgers were ahead, 2 to 1.

"Let's keep it going!" Sterling yelled.

Kenny stepped into the batter's box. He told himself he would do the job this time. He'd drive in Sterling and keep the rally going. The Dodgers finally had Halliday on the run.

But Halliday didn't think so.

He went right after Kenny with a hard pitch inside.

Kenny didn't give an inch. He was still mad at himself for letting Halliday spook him that way last time.

On the next pitch, he hung in there and

took a good swing. He hit the ball solidly, but on the ground.

It had a chance to get through, but the second baseman made a good pickup and threw Kenny out.

Kenny tried not to show any emotion as the Giants hooted and hollered at him. But he was really disappointed.

Kenny hoped that Bunson could come through. The Dodgers needed more than a one-run lead.

But Bunson struck out, trying too hard to hit a long ball.

Harlan kept some hope alive when the first baseman dropped the throw on his grounder. Sterling moved to third. But Eddie took two big swings and then struck out on a called strike.

When he went out to the mound, Bunson really threw hard. He struck out the first two batters, and he got the leadoff batter on an easy grounder.

The last inning was coming up.

The Dodgers hadn't played well, but they were in position to win. For safety, however, they needed some more runs before they went into the bottom of the inning.

But the inning started out all wrong. Danny Sandia hit a long ball—what seemed a sure double. The wind was blowing in, though, and the ball hung up long enough for the fielder to get under it.

Billy followed with a slow roller that the shortstop bobbled. It was a close play at first, but the umpire called Billy out.

Then—suddenly—the luck turned.

Brian Waters came back into the game for Jacob, and he hit an easy grounder to third, but the ball glanced off the third baseman's glove and rolled up his arm. By the time he got a handle on it, he had no chance to get speedy Brian.

Heat poured on the power, but he was forcing the ball.

Henry fouled off a couple of two-strike pitches and finally walked.

Then Sterling hit a pop-up into short right. The second baseman went out and the right fielder charged, but no one could get to it.

Waters had to stop at third, but now the bases were loaded and Kenny had what he wanted: one more chance to drive in some runs.

And one more chance to shut up the Giants.

And some of the Dodgers.

He had actually hit the ball well today, but his luck had been awful. Maybe he was due for a break.

Kenny let an inside pitch go by again. Heat was still trying to scare him.

But Kenny stayed close to the plate and ready.

He caught the next pitch on the nose. He really *drove* the ball to left. It climbed high and long, just the way his big homer had on Wednesday night.

Kenny leaped out of the box and charged toward first, but then he told himself to slow down. He was going to enjoy this one. A grand slam!

He went into his home-run trot, and waved his arms over his head.

But the wind held the ball up.

The left fielder had backed all the way to the fence, but now he came in a few steps.

And he made the catch!

Kenny came to a stop. All the Giants were laughing.

"Hey star, you celebrated a little too soon."

"What a hot dog!"

Kenny trotted toward the dugout. He didn't look at anyone.

He told himself it was okay.

The Dodgers were still ahead. Kenny had given it his best shot. Now he just had to play good defense. The win was still in the Dodgers' pocket.

But David Weight, the Giants' tough-hitting third baseman, was the first batter. Kenny figured he was still mad at himself for the error he had made. Now he would want to do something right.

Maybe Bunson tried too hard to strike him out. He was putting all he had on the ball, and the first two pitches sailed high. He seemed to get his control after that, but on a three-and-two count, Weight held up and the ump called ball four.

Billy ran toward the mound, and Kenny heard him say, "Okay, Burner, don't let that worry you. They've got one of their subs coming up. Just throw strikes.

That turned out to be true. The kid let a couple of strikes go by and then struck out on a weak swing.

And when the center fielder struck out

on a red-hot fastball, things looked very good.

But Halliday was coming up.

Kenny knew what Bunson was thinking.

Kenny ran to the mound this time. "Bunson," he said, "I know you'd like to strike him out, but don't throw *too* hard and get wild."

Bunson nodded, but he overthrew the first couple of pitches, and then, when he tried to let up, he started aiming the ball. He walked Halliday on four pitches.

The Giants' bench really came to life. Cranny was up with the tying run at second—and Bunson was losing his control.

Billy came out to the mound, and Kenny and Henry ran over. "I know, I know," Bunson said. "I won't do that again."

But his timing was suddenly gone. He got a three-and-one pitch over the plate, but he seemed to be listening to all the yelling. Ball four was way outside.

Bases loaded.

Coach Wilkens called time out and walked to the mound.

Kenny was pretty sure he would be pitching. He took a couple of deep breaths and tried to relax. He was going to be up there with all the pressure square on his shoulders.

The coach turned toward him, and Kenny took another deep breath.

But the coach called, "Eddie, come on in. I want you to pitch."

The Giants went nuts.

"He's bringing in Boschi," someone yelled, and everyone cheered and laughed.

"Hey, Doug, it's batting practice time."

Doug Glenn, the tall first baseman, laughed. Kenny could see how sure of himself he was.

It was Eddie who looked nervous. The coach talked to him for a while, and then he walked away.

Eddie took his warm-up pitches.

Kenny thought he looked out of sync, but he wasn't sure what Eddie was doing wrong. He only knew that the ball didn't have much speed.

Boschi took the sign, nodded . . . and threw.

One pitch.

The game was over.

The ball was down the middle, with not

much on it, and Glenn hit it so hard the aluminum bat sounded like a *gonnnnnggg*. The ball landed at the base of the fence, way over Jacob's head, and two runs scored. It was 3 to 2. The Giants had won it.

BOX SCORE, GAME 12

Angel Park Dodgers 2   **Blue Springs Giants 3**

	ab	r	h	rbi		ab	r	h	rbi
White 3b	3	1	1	0	Nugent lf	3	0	0	0
Malone cf	3	0	2	2	Weight 3b	2	1	1	0
Sandoval ss	4	0	0	0	Sanchez ss	1	0	0	0
Bunson p	2	0	0	0	Dodero cf	3	0	0	0
Roper 1b	2	0	0	0	Halliday p	2	1	0	0
Boschi lf	2	0	0	0	Crandall c	1	1	0	0
Reinhold 2b	1	0	1	0	Glenn 1b	3	0	2	3
Bacon c	3	0	0	0	Zonn lf	1	0	0	0
Waters rf	1	0	1	0	Cooper 2b	1	0	0	0
Scott rf	0	1	0	0	Villareal lf	1	0	0	0
Sloan 1b	0	0	0	0	Hausberg rf	1	0	0	0
Sandia 2b	1	0	0	0	Jourdane ss	1	0	0	0
ttl	**22**	**2**	**5**	**2**		**20**	**3**	**3**	**3**

Dodgers 0 0 0 0 2 0—2
Giants 0 1 0 0 0 2—3

★ 5 ★

Big Head

Kenny walked slowly off the field. The Giants were going crazy. Kenny heard his name and knew Cranny was yelling at him, but he didn't look his way.

What he did hear was someone behind him. "What the heck did the coach put Boschi in for?"

Kenny looked around at Danny, who was running in from center field.

"I don't know," Jeff said. "It was *crazy*."

Kenny had been wondering about that too, but he wasn't going to call the coach crazy. He just couldn't figure it out.

"He should have put *you* in," Jeff said, looking at Kenny.

"He should have left Bunson in," Danny said. "The coach is pretty *stupid,* if you ask me."

As the boys reached the dugout, Jacob caught up with them. "Hey, what was the coach thinking about?" he asked.

But Kenny could see that Eddie was sitting on the bench not far away. He had his head down and his hands over his face. "Be quiet," Kenny said to Jacob.

Jacob shot Kenny a dirty look, but he didn't say anything.

The boys lined up and slapped hands with the Giant players. "Don't say anything but 'Good game,' no matter what they say," Coach Wilkens told his players.

And so they went through the line silently, hearing the cocky Giants brag and make fun of the Dodgers. "Tell your coach thanks for letting Boschi pitch," one of the guys yelled.

But Eddie was still sitting on the bench. Kenny thought he was crying. Henry went over and sat down by him and said something, but most of the Dodgers were still complaining.

When the coach called them together, he didn't explain why he had put Eddie in the game, and he didn't make Eddie come over to the group.

He told the players, "Don't put all the blame on one player. Everyone missed some chances out there. But overall, you played a good game. Your defense was as good as in any game this year. You just got beat by a very good team."

That was hard to take. Kenny knew the Giants were good, but he didn't like to admit it.

When the coach walked over to his van to get the soft drinks, no one hurried after him. In fact, some of the players used the chance to start moaning all over again.

"The Giants aren't so great," Billy said. "They lucked out."

"No. We gave it to 'em," Danny said. "Sending Boschi in there was like saying, 'Here, take the game; we don't want it.' "

"He should have put Kenny in," Jeff said again.

But this time Danny let loose. "Who? The little rookie *star*? I think he spent all his time reading the newspaper this week—finding out how great he is." Then he looked Kenny in the face. "If you're so hot, how come you couldn't get a hit today?"

"Lay off, Danny," Jenny said. "We all had trouble hitting Halliday."

"Yeah, but according to the newspaper, Kenny does *everything* right. Isn't that true, Kenny?"

"He didn't write that stuff," Jenny said.

"No. But he sure read it. And I think he *believes* it."

"I *know* he does," Jacob said.

Kenny was stunned. Why would his best friend say something like that?

"Shut up, you guys," Jenny said. "That's stupid. He hit the ball hard. He just had some lousy luck."

But some of the guys were mumbling to each other. He wondered what they were saying.

How many of them agreed with Danny?

Players were finally starting to walk away, heading for the van. Kenny stepped over to Harlan. "What's with Jacob?" he said.

Harlan shrugged.

Jacob walked up to them. "Come on, let's go," he said to Harlan.

"Jacob, what's going on?" Kenny asked.

"Hey, don't ask *us*," Jacob said. "Ask yourself. We're walking home together. You can hang out with your *older* buddies."

Kenny's dad had been waiting during all this time. Now he called to Kenny, "Do you want to ride with me, or walk home with your friends?"

"I'll ride," Kenny said. "Those guys are mad at me."

Mr. Sandoval nodded. "Come on, get in the truck. You can tell me what's going on."

So Kenny walked with his dad to the pickup truck. He told him what Jacob had said.

"Maybe I just ought to tell those guys that the coach called me and *asked* me to practice with Jenny."

"Did the coach ask you not to tell any-one?"

"Sure. But I didn't know it would cause a mess like this. I could just tell Jacob and Harlan not to tell anyone else."

His dad didn't say anything for a moment. He was driving, looking straight ahead. Finally he said, "So is that what you want to do? Do you feel good about that?"

Why did Dad always ask stuff like that?

"I don't know. But I know what *you* think."

"What's that?"

"That I'd be breaking a promise."

"Don't you think you would be?"

"I don't know." Kenny leaned his head back against the dusty old seat cover. "I know what the coach would say."

"What's that?"

"If I tell a couple of guys, the word might get around, and Jenny will feel stupid."

"So is *that* right?"

Kenny thought. His dad had stopped at one of the three stoplights in Angel Park. Mr. Ackerman, who worked at the J. C.

Penney store, crossed in front of the truck and waved at them.

"Jacob does talk a lot," Kenny said. "He might say something even if he promised not to."

"Just like you were thinking about doing."

Dad loved that kind of trap.

Now Kenny didn't know what to do. He had too many things on his mind.

"Dad, why do you think the coach put Eddie in to pitch? He does all right some- times—against the worst teams—but he didn't have a chance against the Giants."

"I don't know, Kenny." His dad stepped on the gas, and the truck growled a little before it moved ahead. "But a coach thinks about a lot of things. Winning is only *one* thing he wants to do. I'll bet he had a good reason for putting Eddie in."

"Danny was really mad about it. He said the coach was stupid."

"Yeah, well, we both know better than that. Besides, Danny's a frustrated kid right now. That's why he's spouting off about you.

He wanted to play shortstop this year, and you beat him out."

"I just did my best."

"I know. But put yourself in his shoes. He's getting a lot of bench time, just when he thought he would be starting. He's a sixth-grader, and you're in third. That's tough on a kid's pride."

"Well, he ought to put himself in *my* shoes. I hated that article in the paper. I don't want everyone thinking I'm supposed to be a hot shot. I don't know if I'm really that good."

"Well, you *do* know that article didn't give you a big head. So don't pay any attention to Danny. Just keep doing your best, and all those guys will come around after a while."

His dad reached out and knocked Kenny's hat off. "And watch out for those high, hard ones," he said.

Kenny didn't think he could laugh, but he did—a little.

"And one last thing," Mr. Sandoval said.

"What?"

"I saw something wrong with the way

Eddie is throwing the ball. Do you want to help him?"

"I guess so." He thought of Eddie sitting on the bench after the game, with his face in his hands. "Yeah, I do."

"Okay. I'll show you what he's doing, and then you can work with him this week."

Turnaround

Kenny crouched as though he were a catcher. "Okay, Eddie, remember the rocking-chair motion. Rock back and get your whole body into the pitch. Don't just throw with your arm."

It was stuff his dad had been teaching Kenny since he was a little kid.

But now Kenny was showing Eddie.

Pop.

"Hey, nice pitch," Kenny yelled. "But make sure your foot plants before you release the ball. You get more power that way."

"Okay," Eddie said, and he threw the ball again.

POP.

"Yeah, that's it. See the difference?"

He threw the ball back to Eddie.

"I'm still afraid to let loose," Eddie said. "I'm afraid I'll throw hard that way, but I won't throw strikes."

"Okay. Here's what my dad tells me. Pretend you're playing catch. Don't aim. Just keep your eye on my glove and use the right motion. You'll throw strikes."

POP!!!!!!!

"Oh, wow." Kenny jerked his glove off and shook his hand. "If you're going to throw like that, I should be using a catcher's mitt."

Eddie smiled even though he tried not to. "Lay off the act," he said.

"Hey, I'm not kidding. That was *hard.* And I didn't have to move my glove to catch it. Just keep practicing the same way."

"Will you keep working with me?"

"Sure. We can work out for a while every day, if you want."

That was on Saturday afternoon. On Monday, after regular practice, and again on Tuesday, Eddie and Kenny practiced together. But they stayed in Kenny's backyard. Eddie said he didn't want to face the other players until he was sure he could pitch better.

Kenny figured Eddie also didn't want to be seen working out with a third-grader.

But Kenny wasn't anxious to see the other players, either. He wanted to prove in the next game that he wasn't getting cocky, but he didn't want to talk about it—or take any more razzing.

Kenny didn't have anyone else to practice with anyway. Jacob and Harlan were avoiding him. And right now he wasn't ready to ask Jenny again.

So on Wednesday evening, Kenny was kind of nervous when he showed up for the game with the A's.

He was doing some warm-up stretches, when he saw Jacob and Harlan walking across the park. He watched as they came closer, and he wondered whether they would say anything. And then, suddenly, the whole thing seemed stupid.

"Hi, you guys," he said.

Harlan said hello, but he glanced at Jacob as though he wasn't sure what he should do.

"Hello, *star*," Jacob said.

Kenny laughed. "Thanks, Jacob. Do you really think I'm that good?"

"*You* do." Jacob wouldn't smile.

But Kenny could see that Harlan almost did.

"I know. I was thinking about trying out for the majors next year, instead of waiting around and playing with a bunch of *youngsters* like you."

"It's not funny, Kenny."

"Yeah, it is. You know I don't think like that."

"Then how come you only practice with the older kids now?"

"I don't. I just—"

"You've practiced with Eddie every night this week."

Kenny nodded. "Okay, but there's a reason for that. My dad saw something Eddie was doing wrong when he pitched the other night."

"One pitch?"

"He saw him warm up too. He told me some stuff I could show him so he—"

"Because you're the rookie star. And you know *everything*."

But Harlan finally spoke up. "Come on, Jacob. Kenny said it was stuff his dad told him."

"Why are you sticking up for him, Harlan?" Jacob said. "You're the one he's been badmouthing."

"What?" Kenny said. "What are you talking about? I never said anything bad about Harlan."

"You told Jenny that Harlan wasn't good enough for you to practice with."

"Oh."

Suddenly Kenny knew he was in real trouble. He also knew why his friends had been so mad at him. "Who told you that?"

"Jenny's friend. Cindy. She said she was standing right there when you said it."

Kenny looked at Harlan, but he couldn't think of what to say.

"*See,*" Jacob said, "you're not even denying it."

"Look, I said that," Kenny said. "But I was making it up. I was making an excuse so I could give Jenny a reason . . . for asking her to . . ."

But he knew he couldn't finish the sentence.

"Because you think you're too good to practice with us now. You want to spend all your time with the fifth- and sixth-graders."

"No way. I—"

"So you don't want to practice with me, huh?"

Kenny spun around. There was Jenny. Kenny wondered how much she had heard.

"No, I . . . I mean . . ."

"Jacob, I'll tell you what's going on," Jenny said. She walked over to him. She came close, so she was looking down at Jacob. "Last week Kenny did ask me to practice with him."

"I know that."

"But you don't know why. The coach told him to."

Jenny looked at Kenny, but Kenny looked down at the grass. He wasn't going to admit that.

"I know why the coach did it—but it's not important. Or at least I'm not telling you guys. But you don't have to think Kenny's acting like a hot shot."

Jacob looked at Kenny. He looked unsure of himself now. "Did the coach really tell you to practice with Jenny?"

Kenny glanced at Jenny and then back at Jacob. He finally just shrugged.

"I'll bet the coach also made him promise not to say anything about it," Jenny said.

"Why would he do that?"

"None of your business." But Jenny was grinning.

"Look, that doesn't make any sense," Jacob said. "Why would the coach—"

"It doesn't matter why, Jacob," Harlan said.

Jacob was the one who didn't know what to say now.

"We promised we'd all stick together this year—the three rookies," Harlan said.

"I know. But I thought he was the one breaking the promise."

"Well, he wasn't. I've been telling you that all week."

Kenny smiled. "Gee, Jacob," he said. "I'm not really such a bad guy. My mom likes me."

Jacob suddenly couldn't resist. He let that gap-toothed grin sneak out—just a little. "That doesn't prove anything," he said. "Cranny's mom probably likes him."

"Nah. I doubt it," Jenny said, and they all laughed.

And Kenny knew things were okay with Jacob again.

But Kenny still had to know one thing. "How did you know?" he asked Jenny.

She took a couple of steps away and motioned Kenny over. Then she whispered in his ear, "How dumb do you think I am? I had that talk with the coach, and two days later you come up and want to practice with me. I saw right through that stuff about Harlan not catching the ball."

"So how come you went to the park with me anyway?"

"Because you're so cute, Kenny."

She patted him on the head.

"Lay off," Kenny said. And he felt himself go red.

★ 7 ★

Stiff Arm

Kenny felt better to have one problem straightened out. But the team still seemed down. He knew everyone still felt lousy about losing to the Giants.

And Danny was still on Kenny's back:

"I hope the 'rookie star' can hit the ball today—so he can *lead* us on to victory and get his picture in the paper again."

Kenny was surprised that Bunson was the one who told Danny to lay off. But he was just as surprised when Billy and Jeff laughed at Danny's wisecracks.

Kenny wasn't sure whether any of the guys were really buying Danny's idea that Kenny had gotten a big head, but he did know that something wasn't right with the team.

When Sterling popped up in the first inning, Jeff yelled, "Come on, Sterling, that pitch wasn't even in the strike zone."

Kenny followed with a single—which shut Danny up for the moment. But Bunson struck out, and Kenny heard someone shout from the dugout, "Bunson. Quit swinging for the fences."

It just wasn't the way the players usually talked to each other. Everyone was suddenly seeing everyone else's mistakes.

Kenny was pitching, and he got the side out, but the Dodgers failed to score again in the second inning.

"What's going on?" Bunson yelled to everyone. "We *killed* these guys the last two times." He sounded mad—maybe at himself.

But nothing changed. Kenny pitched well. He would have gotten the A's out in order again, but Billy let a third strike get by him, and the runner beat the throw to first. Then Jenny dropped a throw from Henry on a ground ball.

The Dodgers were lucky to get out of the inning with the score still nothing to nothing.

The top of the order was coming up for the Dodgers in the third. "Let's get it going," Billy barked at everyone. "Let's start *playing ball.*"

The A's had been quiet at first. But now they were tossing the ball around the horn and talking it up:

"We can *beat* these guys. We're as good as they are," the second baseman yelled, and the whole team cheered.

When Henry White hit a sharp grounder toward the hole at short, the Dodgers jumped up and cheered. But the A's shortstop got to it, spun, and made a good throw. Earlier in the season, she never would have managed that.

Now the A's were feeling cocky. "Nice play," the catcher yelled. "We're not as good as these guys. We're *better.*"

The infield tossed the ball around the horn again. And then the catcher looked Sterling in the eye and said, "You didn't think we could play this good, did you?"

Kenny watched Sterling. Sterling didn't say anything, but he dug in as though he was getting ready to hit the ball downtown.

He swung for the fences. But he topped the ball and sent an easy grounder to first base.

Kenny was coming up.

"Get it going, Kenny," Coach Wilkens called out.

And Kenny tried.

But he went after a ball that was outside. He tried to hold up, but he was too late. The ball dribbled off his bat and rolled to the pitcher—who threw him out with no trouble.

Danny yelled, "What kind of swing was that, *star*?"

The A's seemed amazed by what was happening. They picked up the chant.

"Hey, *star*, you been reading the paper too much?"

"Hey, star, the paper said you were better than that."

As Kenny walked to the mound he had to listen to the whole team—and plenty in the stands—work him over.

He told himself it didn't bother him.

But he knew it did.

The first batter to come up in the third for the A's was the shortstop. She looked a lot more confident than she had all season. Kenny threw a pretty good fastball, but she met it and drove a high fly to left.

Boschi went back a few steps and then braked and charged in again. He ran hard, but he couldn't get to it. The ball dropped in front of him and then skipped on by.

An easy out suddenly turned into a double.

"Eddie, you idiot!" Danny yelled from the bench. "Are you going to lose another game for us?"

Kenny saw the coach walk to the dugout, and he knew Danny was getting chewed out. But Jeff had some things to say, too.

"I can't believe that guy," he mumbled, as he kicked at the dirt. "Eddie can't do anything right."

Kenny walked over to Jeff. "It's easy to misjudge a fly ball," he said. "We've all done it. Don't say anything to him."

Jeff didn't want to hear that. He walked

away. Kenny knew how frustrated he was.
A loss to the A's—after the one to the
Giants—would put the Dodgers in real
trouble.

And things didn't get better when the
runner moved to third on a passed ball.

"What are you doing, Billy?" Jeff yelled.

Kenny bore down on the next batter and
got a strikeout.

That eased some of the pressure.

And then Jared Bessant, the A's best hitter, came up and hit a ground ball that
Henry fielded. He looked the runner back
to third, and then he made a perfect throw
to first.

But just as things started to look better,
Kenny let a pitch get away from him. He
tried to throw his curve, but it hung—stayed
right out over the plate.

The little center fielder slammed it. He
must have hit the hardest shot of his life.

The ball jolted off his bat. Kenny spun
around and watched it streak over the fence
on a line.

Kenny looked at the sky for a moment,
and then at the ground. He didn't want to
look at the players—on either team.

The A's were all screaming about the "rookie star" not being so great. But Kenny was more worried about what his own team was thinking.

Kenny did get the next batter—on a foul tick that Billy held on to for a third strike.

But as Kenny walked toward the dugout, Billy said, "What's going on, Kenny? That pitch had *nothing* on it."

"All right, now that's enough!"

Everyone spun around and saw the coach coming toward them.

"What's *with* you kids? You lose one game, and suddenly you're all blaming each other for everything that goes wrong. If I hear one more player knock his own teammate, I'm going to tell the ump to give the game to the A's."

The Dodger players were silent. No one would even look at Coach Wilkens.

Then Jenny said, "Come on, you guys, let's not blow the whole season. Let's play baseball and lay off all this other stuff."

No one said too much, but something began to turn.

Bunson watched what he was doing and got a walk. Jenny got a break on a blooper down the right field line that dropped for a single.

Suddenly the A's seemed to lose their confidence. The second baseman, who had made some good plays earlier, let a ball go between his legs, and two runs scored. By the time the inning was over, Brian and Henry had each driven in another run, and the score was 4 to 2.

Kenny ended the inning with a fly to left, and he was disappointed, but no one said anything about it.

When he got the side out in order, some of the players slapped him on the back. He could feel the spirit coming back.

And yet, Kenny knew, not all the problems had been solved. There were some bad feelings that still had to be settled if the team was going to come together again.

And he knew one thing that might help. It was a plan that could backfire, though.

But then the Dodgers started hitting again and got three more runs. Kenny thought it was time to take a chance.

He walked over to Coach Wilkens and said, "Coach, my arm really stiffened up on me while we were sitting there. Maybe I better not pitch anymore today."

"Stiffened? Are you sure?" the coach asked.

"Yeah. It feels really tight, Coach."

The coach looked doubtful.

"Maybe," Kenny said, "this would be a good chance for Eddie to get some more work—now that we have a good lead. He's been pitching a lot better this week."

Coach Wilkens nodded. "He did look good on Monday."

"I think he should get another chance."

"Yeah, I was thinking the same thing. But I was going to wait one more inning and just let him get the last three outs."

"He'll do fine for two innings. He was really whistling them in the last few days." Kenny made a pitching motion with his arm.

"I thought your arm was stiff," the coach said, smiling.

"Oh, it is, Coach. It's really killing me."

And Kenny smiled back.

★ 8 ★

Rocking Chair

Kenny saw the reaction when the coach called Eddie in to pitch. Danny was heading out to play right field, but when he heard the coach, he spun around and said, "Oh, *no!*"

The coach pointed his finger at Danny, but he didn't say a word. Kenny knew what it meant, and he was sure Danny did too: "Cool it, Danny."

No one else was going to say anything, but Kenny saw Jeff and Bunson walk toward each other. They met at second base and talked, quietly. Bunson had his hands on his hips and he looked disgusted.

The good feeling that had been coming back to the team was suddenly gone.

Eddie ran out to the mound, and he took his first warm-up pitch. But he looked stiff as a scarecrow. He was going back to his old motion.

Kenny yelled, "Eddie! Remember what you've been practicing."

But Eddie was too nervous, or was just trying too hard. He made another awkward pitch. The ball bounced in the dirt in front of the plate.

By the time he had finished his warm-ups, the A's were laughing and yelling. They were expecting to pound poor Eddie.

And the first batter did exactly that. He was the substitute right fielder and not one of the A's good hitters, but he slammed the first pitch up the middle for a single.

Jeff looked over at Bunson again, and they both shook their heads.

Kenny knew he had to do something.

"Coach," he yelled. "Let me talk to Eddie for a minute."

Kenny was already running from the dugout toward the mound.

But halfway there he heard the umpire call, "Hey, young man, you can't do that."

Kenny stopped. Quickly he yelled, "Eddie, don't throw with your arm. Remember. Use your whole body. Rocking chair. Plant your foot and follow through."

Eddie nodded. Kenny hurried off the field.

Eddie took a deep breath, and he got his sign from the catcher. But then he turned and walked off the mound.

He stood for a moment, looking up at the sky. Kenny knew he was trying to get an image of what he had to do.

This time, when he went back to the pitching rubber, he took another breath, and then let his arm—his whole body—rock back and forth a couple of times. His eye was right on Billy's glove.

When he brought the ball back, he hardly looked like the same guy. Those flying arms had turned into part of his body, and his motion was smooth and strong. He planted his front foot and lashed the ball through.

The ball popped into Billy's glove and the A's leadoff hitter didn't even move.

"*Steee-rike,*" the umpire barked.

Billy came up grinning. "Good pitch," he yelled.

Eddie nodded, and then he fired the same pitch again.

The kid swung this time, but he swung late. Suddenly Eddie had some power behind his pitches.

Eddie's next pitch was a little outside, but with two strikes, the batter got anxious and swung anyway.

Thump.

The ball hit the catcher's mitt, and the batter got nothing but air.

"*Steee-rike three.* The batter's out."

Billy ran halfway to the mound with the ball. "All *right,* Eddie," he yelled. "Way to fire. Keep it up."

Bunson was smiling, and so was Jeff. Kenny looked out at Danny, who was shaking his head as though he didn't believe it.

But Eddie made believers of everyone—including the A's—when he struck out the next batter, the good-hitting left fielder.

When Jared Bessant came up, Kenny could see that Eddie's confidence was strong, but he also knew what a good hitter Bessant was. This would be the real test.

Eddie couldn't just throw hard down the middle. He had to show some control and prove he could move the ball around.

Eddie seemed to know that too.

The first pitch was down in the strike zone. Bessant had a good swing, but he fouled the pitch off.

Eddie looked a little concerned.

"Eddie," Kenny yelled. Eddie looked over. "Just think of that motion. Rocking chair."

Eddie nodded, and then he rocked back and fired a fastball that was barely outside.

But Bessant was smart. He let the pitch go by.

Eddie came inside the next time, and Bessant got around on the pitch. He drilled the ball down the left field line—but foul.

Eddie took another long breath. He got the ball back, stared in at Billy's mitt, and nodded. He used his full motion and seemed to let go with another heater. But he used his change-up grip, and the ball floated up to the plate.

Bessant swung early and barely ticked the ball.

It rolled in front of the plate and Billy jumped out and snapped it to Harlan. Bessant was out before he got halfway to first.

When the Dodgers ran off the field, they were all yelling to Eddie, telling him what a great job he had done. And Eddie was grinning.

But he didn't jump around. He looked more confident than excited.

He even went out and got a good hit, helping the Dodgers pick up another pair of runs.

When he went back to the mound, he closed off the A's without any problem. He looked almost as good as Bunson.

The Dodgers finally had themselves three good pitchers—just what they were going to need as it got closer to the end of the season.

Kenny felt great. He liked seeing everyone so happy.

And the team celebrated more than they usually would after beating the A's.

Everyone seemed to know that something important had happened. The players were all patting each other on the back, talking to each other like friends again.

The Dodgers gave the A's a cheer, and they lined up and slapped hands with them.

The coach called them together after that, as always.

He told them he was proud of them for the way they played when they had to. "But to tell you the truth, I'm still worried. I'm not sure we're a team yet."

The players got very quiet.

"Eddie did a good job today, and so you're all happy. But what if he had given it his best shot and still had problems? Would you be yelling at him instead of slapping him on the back?"

The coach was looking right at Danny.

"Every one of you messes up at times. But what you need is someone pulling for you, not someone telling you how bad you are. I put Eddie in the last game to give him the experience of pitching in a tough situation. He didn't get the out, but he deserved better treatment than you kids gave him."

Kenny looked around. He could see that some of the guys were feeling ashamed of themselves.

"And there's something else. I've watched you kids ride Kenny Sandoval all week. He's a good player, and he always gives his best shot. But just because the local paper decides to write a story about him, some of you made up your minds he's a hot dog."

Kenny was too embarrassed to look at anyone.

"Do you know that he asked to be taken out of this game so that Eddie could pitch? Is that what a hot dog would do?"

"Coach," Eddie said.

"Yes."

"Kenny's been working with me all week. His dad picked up some mistakes I was making in my pitching motion, and Kenny has been helping me change the way I throw. That's why I did so much better today."

"*All right*," the coach said. "Now, you tell me, players, whether Kenny Sandoval has a big head. You tell me whether you had any right to get on his back."

Everyone was quiet. Everyone knew what the answer was, but no one said anything.

Then Jenny spoke up.

"I think he's a nice boy, Coach," she said. "His mom told me that he helps with the dishes."

The kids cracked up. Everyone laughed—hard. Even the coach.

But when the players all finally stopped laughing and stood up, no one knew exactly what to do.

And then Danny slapped hands with Kenny. And everyone else did the same—the whole team.

Jacob and Harlan waited until the end and gave him one of their high-fives. Then Jacob said, "Hey, Kenny, do you want to walk home with Harlan and me?"

"No way," Kenny said.

Jacob looked surprised. "Are you still mad at us?"

"No. But my dad's waiting. He said he'd take me out for a hamburger—and then take me swimming."

"Oh. Well, we'll see you later then."

"And he wondered if you guys wanted to go with us."

Jacob's freckled face lit up. "That'd be good," he said.

And Harlan added, "Yeah. We rookies gotta stick together."

BOX SCORE, GAME 13

Angel Park Dodgers   9   **Paseo A's   2**

	ab	r	h	rbi		ab	r	h	rbi
White 3b	4	0	2	3	McConnell ss	3	1	1	0
Malone cf	4	0	0	0	Boston lf	3	0	0	0
Sandoval p	3	0	1	0	Bessant 3b	2	0	0	0
Bunson ss	3	3	2	0	Sullivan cf	3	1	1	2
Roper 1b	2	1	1	0	Santos 1b	3	0	0	0
Reinhold 2b	0	1	0	0	Smith c	0	0	0	0
Boschi lf	3	0	1	1	Watrous p	1	0	0	0
Bacon c	3	2	1	1	Oshima 2b	1	0	0	0
Waters rf	3	0	1	1	Trout rf	1	0	0	0
Sloan 1b	2	2	2	1	Chavez 2b	1	0	0	0
Scott 2b	2	0	1	0	Powell c	2	0	0	0
Sandia ss	1	0	0	0	De Klein rf	1	0	1	0
ttl	**30**	**9**	**12**	**7**		**21**	**2**	**3**	**2**

Dodgers	0	0	0	4	3	2—9
A's	0	0	2	0	0	0—2

League standings after three games:
(Second half of season)

Reds	2–1
Giants	2–1
Dodgers	2–1
Mariners	2–1
A's	1–2
Padres	0–3

First game scores:

Dodgers	13	Padres	4
Giants	9	Mariners	6
Reds	11	A's	8

Second game scores:

Giants	3	Dodgers	2
Mariners	5	Reds	4
A's	12	Padres	11

Third games scores:

Dodgers	9	A's	2
Mariners	4	Padres	1
Reds	4	Giants	2

DEAN HUGHES has written many books for children including the popular *Nutty* stories and *Jelly's Circus*. He has also published such works of literary fiction for young adults as the highly acclaimed *Family Pose*. When he's not attending Little League games, Mr. Hughes devotes his full time to writing. He lives in Utah with his wife and family.

ANGEL PARK ALL-STARS #1

Making the Team
by Dean Hughes
**They aced the tryouts—but can they win
over their teammates?**

Kenny, Jacob, and Harlan are the three youngest
Little Leaguers to make the Angel Park Dodgers.
They're all anxious to prove themselves to the older
guys, but they haven't counted on the antagonism
of team slugger (and bully!) Rodney Bunson. He'll
do *anything* to stay on top. Can the rookies survive
Rodney's version of hardball? Can the Dodgers?

FIRST TIME IN PRINT!

BULLSEYE BOOKS PUBLISHED BY ALFRED A. KNOPF

ANGEL PARK ALL-STARS #2

Big Base Hit
by Dean Hughes
He really needs one—or he may be off the team!

His buddies Kenny and Jacob, the other third graders on the team, have already gotten their hits. Harlan knows he won't really feel like an Angel Park Dodger until he gets his. But no dice. The harder he tries, the worse it gets. Soon everyone's starting to worry—especially Harlan. What if he *never* gets a hit? What if he doesn't belong on the team after all?

FIRST TIME IN PRINT!

BULLSEYE BOOKS PUBLISHED BY ALFRED A. KNOPF

ANGEL PARK ALL-STARS #3

Winning Streak
by Dean Hughes
**It's been great so far—but
is their luck finally running out?**

They were hotter than hot the first four games of the season, but now it looks as though Kenny and the Angel Park Dodgers are headed for a slump. The third-grade rookies try all kinds of tricks to change their luck, but when they continue to strike out, zany, brainy Jacob decides to take drastic action. But what if his wild scheme fails? What if he *can't* get the Dodgers back on the winning track?

FIRST TIME IN PRINT!

BULLSEYE BOOKS PUBLISHED BY ALFRED A. KNOPF

ANGEL PARK ALL-STARS #4

What a Catch!
by Dean Hughes
This may be Brian's last chance to prove himself to the team!

Brian, the smallest sixth grader on the Angel Park Dodgers, gives baseball all he's got. But lately that just isn't enough. After he flubs a catch that sends him crashing, he decides he's the worst player on the Little League team—and that just makes him more nervous. Will he ever be able to prove to the others—and especially to himself—that he really *can* play ball?

FIRST TIME IN PRINT!

BULLSEYE BOOKS PUBLISHED BY ALFRED A. KNOPF